FINCASTLE LIBRARY
11 ACADEMY ST.
P. O. BOX 129
FINCASTLE, VA 24090

A Note to Parents

Read to your child...

★ Reading aloud is one of the best ways to develop your child's love of reading. Read together at least 20 minutes each day.

★ Laughter is contagious! Read with feeling. Show your child that reading is fun.

★ Take time to answer questions your child may have about the story. Linger over pages that interest your child.

...and your child will read to you.

★ Follow cues from your child to know when he wants to join in the reading.

★ Support your young reader. Give him a word whenever he asks for it.

★ Praise your child as he progresses. Your encouraging words will build his confidence.

You can help your Level 1 reader.

★ Reading begins with knowing how a book works. Show your child the title and where the story begins.

★ Ask your child to find picture clues on each page. Talk about what is happening in the story.

★ Point to the words as you read so your child can make the connection between the print and the story.

★ Ask your child to point to words she knows.

★ Let your child supply the rhyming words.

Most of all, enjoy your reading time together!

—**Bernice Cullinan, Ph.D.,**
Professor of Reading, New York University

Published by Reader's Digest Children's Books
Reader's Digest Road, Pleasantville, NY U.S.A. 10570-7000 and
Reader's Digest Children's Publishing Limited,
The Ice House, 124-126 Walcot Street, Bath UK BA1 5BG
Copyright © 1999 Reader's Digest Children's Publishing, Inc.
All rights reserved. Reader's Digest Children's Books is a trademark and
Reader's Digest and All-Star Readers are registered trademarks of
The Reader's Digest Association, Inc. Fisher-Price trademarks are used
under license from Fisher-Price, Inc., a subsidiary of
Mattel, Inc., East Aurora, NY 14052 U.S.A.
©2000 Mattel, Inc. All Rights Reserved.
Printed in Hong Kong.
10 9 8 7

Library of Congress Cataloging-in-Publication Data

Hall, Kirsten.
　　My best friend / by Kirsten Hall ; illustrated by Chris Demarest.
　　　　p. cm. — (All-star readers. Level 1)
　　Summary: A boy describes his best friend, his puppy.
　　ISBN 1-57584-913-5
　　[1. Dogs—Fiction. 2. Pets—Fiction. 3. Best friends—Fiction. 4. Friendship—Fiction. 5.
Stories in rhyme.] I. Demarest, Chris L., ill. II. Title. III. Series.

PZ8.3.H146 Mv 2001
[E]—dc21
　　　　　　　　　　　　　　　　　　　　　　　　　　　　　　　　　2001041832

0 1191 0324279 6

My Best Friend

by **Kirsten Hall**
illustrated by **Chris Demarest**

FINCASTLE LIBRARY
11 ACADEMY ST.
P. O. BOX 129
FINCASTLE, VA 24090

All-Star Readers®

Reader's Digest Children's Books™
Pleasantville, New York • Montréal, Québec

I love my friend.

He loves me, too.

He's my best friend.

Can you guess who?

He's not too big.

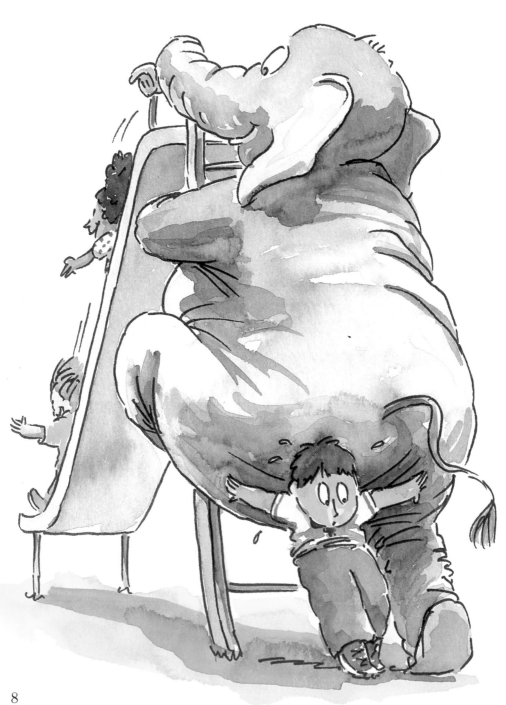

He's not too small.

He does not talk or sing at all.

He loves to jump.

He loves to run.

He loves to play.

He's always fun.

He loves the park.

He loves to chase.

He always beats me
when we race.

FINCASTLE LIBRARY

He always greets me
at my door.

He's always hungry.

More! More! More!

He'll be my dog
when I grow up.

So, did you guess?

My friend's a pup!

Color in the star next to each word you can read.

☆ a	☆ greets	☆ pup
☆ all	☆ grow	☆ race
☆ always	☆ guess	☆ run
☆ at	☆ he	☆ sing
☆ be	☆ he'll	☆ small
☆ beats	☆ he's	☆ so
☆ best	☆ hungry	☆ talk
☆ big	☆ I	☆ the
☆ can	☆ jump	☆ to
☆ chase	☆ love	☆ too
☆ did	☆ me	☆ up
☆ does	☆ more	☆ we
☆ dog	☆ my	☆ when
☆ door	☆ not	☆ who
☆ friend	☆ or	☆ you
☆ friend's	☆ park	
☆ fun	☆ play	

FINCASTLE LIBRARY
11 ACADEMY ST.
P. O. BOX 129
FINCASTLE, VA 24090